KT-102-677

This book belongs to:

. . . .

I celebrated World Book Day
2020 with this gift from my local
bookseller and Canongate.

#ShareAStory

CELEBRATE STORIES. LOVE READING.

This book has been specially created and published to celebrate **World Book Day. World Book Day** is a charity funded by publishers and booksellers in the UK and Ireland. Our mission is to offer every child and young person the opportunity to read and love books by giving you the chance to have a book of your own. To find out more, and for loads of fun activities and reading recommendations to help you to keep reading, visit **worldbookday.com**

World Book Day in the UK and Ireland is also made possible by generous sponsorship from National Book Tokens and support from authors and illustrators.

World Book Day works in partnership with a number of charities, who are all working to encourage a love of reading for pleasure.

The National Literacy Trust is an independent charity that encourages children and young people to enjoy reading. Just 10 minutes of reading every day can make a big difference to how well you do at school and to how successful you could be in life. **literacytrust.org.uk**

The Reading Agency inspires people of all ages and backgrounds to read for pleasure and empowerment. They run the Summer Reading Challenge in partnership with libraries; they also support reading groups in schools and libraries all year round. Find out more and join your local library. **summerreadingchallenge.org.uk**

BookTrust is the UK's largest children's reading charity. Each year they reach 3.4 million children across the UK with books, resources and support to help develop a love of reading. **booktrust.org.uk**

World Book Day also facilitates fundraising for:

Book Aid International, an international book donation and library development charity. Every year, they provide one million books to libraries and schools in communities where children would otherwise have little or no opportunity to read. **bookaid.org**

Read for Good, who motivate children in schools to read for fun through its sponsored read, which thousands of schools run on World Book Day and throughout the year. The money raised provides new books and resident storytellers in all the children's hospitals in the UK. **readforgood.org**

Matt Haig

Evie in the
JUNGLE

Illustrated by Emily Gravett

CANONGATE

First published in Great Britain in 2020
by Canongate Books Ltd,
14 High Street, Edinburgh EH1 1TE

canongate.co.uk

1

British Library Cataloguing-in-Publication Data
A catalogue record for this book is available on
request from the British Library

ISBN 978 1 83885 075 3

Typeset in Bembo by
Palimpsest Book Production Ltd, Falkirk, Stirlingshire

Printed and bound in Great Britain
by Clays Ltd, Elcograf S.p.A.

MIX
Paper from
responsible sources
FSC
www.fsc.org   FSC® C018072

Evie the Superstar

vie Navarro opened the front door and saw a crowd of photographers and journalists.

'EVIE! EVIE! CAN WE ASK A FEW QUESTIONS?'

'EVIE! WHAT IS IT LIKE TO BE FAMOUS?'

'EVIE! HERE'S A DOG! CAN YOU READ ITS THOUGHTS?'

Evie stood there feeling dizzy and lightheaded. 'Um, um . . . I'm sorry – I've got to go.'

Evie was a superstar.

That's what her best friend Ramesh said.

'You are a superstar,' he had told her the previous Tuesday, while eating a hummus and falafel sandwich on their favourite bench at Lofting High.

But she wasn't really. Well, Evie didn't think so. She wasn't a celeb or anything.

It was just that a lot of people had heard of her.

She had been in newspapers, and on TV. She had been on the cover of the world-famous *Nature* magazine, and she had over 200,000 followers on Instagram, even though she had only ever posted two photos (one of a sunset and one of an endangered leatherback sea turtle). And every morning the crowd of journalists at her door grew bigger.

The reason for all this fame and unwanted attention was because Evie had a special talent.

The talent now had an official name, given by scientists.

Inter-species two-way telepathic animal communication.

Or, to put it another way, she could talk to animals. *With her mind.*

She heard what animals were thinking and

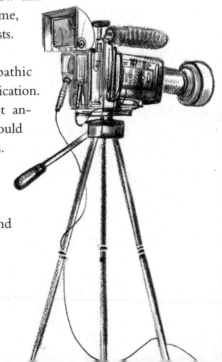

could chat to them without even moving her lips.

And though she had kept this skill secret for a very long time, now everybody knew about it.

She had solved a crime with it. And there was lots of proof. On TV. On YouTube. In magazines. Communicating with dolphins at her local zoo. Getting mice to march in a line. Asking rabbits for directions to their burrow. Telling a bearded dragon to change the TV channel, and conducting an interview with a seagull.

There were thousands of strangers on the internet calling her a freak, so Evie had been locking herself away in her bedroom and reading. The book she had been reading most was called *Animals of the Amazon*, by Professor Abigail García. It was amazing. Full of astonishing facts, and written by a biologist who actually worked in the Amazon, in Peru, finding new species and helping to save the rainforest. Abigail García was on the front cover, smiling and waving in front of the trees, with a parrot on her shoulder.

Evie was holding that exact book in her hands as she stared out at all the shouting reporters.

'EVIE! EVIE! GIVE US A SMILE!'

'I'm sorry. I'm just tired—'

'EVIE! WHAT DO YOU SAY TO PEOPLE WHO SAY YOU ARE A FAKE?'

'I'd say ask the scientists who have confirmed I am not—'

'EVIE! DO YOU THINK FAME IS GOING TO YOUR HEAD?'

'I'd rather not be famous, to be honest—'

'EVIE! EVIE! EVIE!'

Evie's dog Scruff came to her side.

'GET A LIFE!' he barked at the reporters. 'LEAVE EVIE ALONE!'

But the reporters didn't speak dog, and so they carried on doing what they were doing.

Then Evie's dad came and slammed the front door in the reporters' faces.

'Evie, I told you not to answer the door . . .'

'I forgot.'

'She forgot,' said Scruff, in her defence. 'She *is* quite forgetful. I mean, I haven't had a tummy rub all morning.'

'Scruff, I've just woken up. You had forty-eight tummy rubs yesterday. At least.'

'You say that like there can be such a thing as too many tummy rubs,' said Scruff. 'And, well, there can't.'

A Big and Dangerous Place

A little later, over breakfast, Evie's dad had an idea about how to deal with all this unwanted attention.

'It's the school holidays next week. We need to get away for a while,' he said, pulling the blinds down to stop the reporters from looking in. 'What do you think?'

Evie nodded. 'One hundred per cent agree.'

'Where would you like to go?'

Evie looked down at the book she was holding. 'How about the Amazon? I'd like to go back. I know we were there when I was little, when you and Mum worked there, but I can't remember it except in dreams. Maybe we could make those dreams real?'

Her dad looked worried for a moment. Then he smiled. 'You are your mother's child. But the Amazon is a big and dangerous place. Are you sure? And what about Scruff?'

Scruff was lying in his basket.

'Would you like to go and stay with Granny Flora?' Evie asked the dog.

'Yes,' Scruff said. 'Yes, I would. I get to sleep in her bed and she gives me human food. Including pizza. I like pizza. I know I shouldn't but I do. Pizza is good. Can I go right now?'

'Scruff would be fine at Granny Flora's,' Evie told her dad.

'Okay. But it's the *Amazon*.'

Evie sighed. She knew all about the Amazon. Not just from her dreams but also from books. She knew that one out of ten animals that exist on Earth can be found in the rainforest. And that many of them are dangerous – poison dart frogs, wandering spiders and sleek, prowling spotted jaguars.

But she also knew that more dangerous than all of those creatures were human beings. She knew the rainforest was under attack. Humans destroy enough rainforest to fill thirty football pitches every minute.

'I'm sure. I want to go there and think about doing something useful. I want to help fight climate change. I want to protect animals. This might help me do that.'

'Do you want to visit the Brazilian rainforest?'

Evie shook her head. Her mum had died in the Brazilian rainforest.

'No. Not yet. I've been thinking about Peru,' said Evie.

'Wow. You really have thought about this. But I am worried.'

'There's a surprise.'

'I'm sorry, Evie, but it's not the safest place for a holiday. Are you sure you don't want to go to Mallorca? Or the South of France? Or . . . *Cornwall*? Cornwall's nice.'

'A riverboat cruise would be safe,' she suggested. 'And I could meet some pink river dolphins. I've done my research. There's one called Ernesto's River Adventures. It's a small boat. Just a few passengers.'

'Well, okay. I'll look into it. But maybe we should sneak away to Granny Flora's until we go. Just to get away from all this noise.'

'Thanks, Dad!' said Evie.

'Thanks!' said Scruff, closing his eyes and thinking of all that pizza.

Evie's dad smiled. 'But I can't promise pink river dolphins!'

Riding the River

The riverboat cruise had been a great idea.

Evie and her dad were having an amazing time in Peru, sailing down the river.

She had exchanged thoughts with a (gentle) manatee and a (grumpy) giant otter and had had a shocking conversation with an electric eel, whose thoughts zapped and jolted about so fast Evie got a headache. They had:

- visited a nature reserve known as the 'Jungle of Mirrors' where the backwaters were so still that they could see their reflections;
- spotted a three-toed sloth in the trees and Evie had mind-chatted sleepily with her;
- met more species of monkeys and birds than even Evie had known existed;
- and finally caught a glimpse of a deadly-looking jaguar between the trees.

The glimpse of the jaguar had been far too short for Evie's liking, and she hadn't been able to pick up on its thoughts.

'I'd love to be face to face with a jaguar,' Evie said.

Her dad went pale. 'Maybe we could get a cat when we get home,' he said. 'A nice *small* cat. I mean, cats are cats. I'm sure Scruff wouldn't mind.'

'He would mind. He thinks cats are evil. He thinks cats are in a plot to take over the world and then make dogs their slaves. And anyway, I would *love* to talk with a jaguar.'

'Jaguars are killers,' her dad said.

'But, Dad, so are humans. I mean, technically. And you're a human and I still talk to you.'

'Yes. But unlike a jaguar, I'm not going to bite your head off. Even if I got *really* angry.'

Evie sighed. 'Dad, that's prejudiced. Jaguars rarely kill humans.'

Her dad decided to change the subject. 'Shall we look for some pink river dolphins?'

'Sure,' said Evie. 'It's a shame we haven't seen any yet.'

'There is still time!' said Gerry, a friendly, twinkly-eyed American man with wild grey hair, who was one of the few other passengers on board the boat.

'Oh yes,' said his red-cheeked wife, Barbara, looking through her binoculars across the river. 'We should hopefully see them as we get closer to Iquitos City.'

Iquitos City. Their final destination.

It is the largest city in the world that you can't get to by road. You either have to fly there, or get a boat.

The riverboat was captained by a hairy man called Ernesto who drank and passed around a lot of bottles of Inca Kola, a local soft drink — a sweet, slightly sickly liquid that Evie thought tasted like melted ice cream. She liked it and she also liked the food. They had stopped at a hut beside the river that sold something called tacu tacu, a kind of fried dumpling that was sticky and totally yummy.

As Evie bit into the tacu tacu, and wondered why they weren't sold all over the world, they

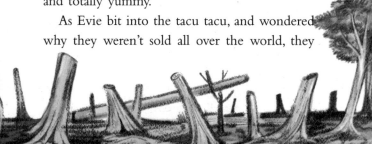

set sail again. She leant over the side of the boat, looking for amazing river creatures to chat with, in the hope of seeing a pink river dolphin.

The jungle was incredible. The vast, wide brown-green river. The rubber trees lining its banks. The parrots flying overhead. The buzz of insects and the distant squawks and squeals of unseen animals far away in the trees. It felt like life itself.

There were some sad sights along the way, though, as they got a bit closer to Iquitos City. Evie saw stretches of empty dead land where the forest had been destroyed. She saw smoke rising above the jungle where developers had set fire to the trees in order to clear the land.

'Isn't it terrible,' sighed Barbara, 'what people are doing to this place?'

And then it happened.

Right there, in that moment of sadness.

Gerry pointed to the river. 'Look! In the water! Just below the surface!'

And Evie saw it. A rising pinkness.

Could it be? Could it possibly be?

Yes.

'A dolphin!'

The Pink Dolphins
of Peru

E vie quickly realised there wasn't just one
dolphin.

There was another.

And another.

And another.

And another.

And . . .

SIX!

SIX DOLPHINS!

They burst out of the water, one after the other.
As pink as Evie had hoped they would be.

Evie remembered reading in *Animals of the
Amazon* that when the dolphins were young they
were a normal dolphin grey, but by the time they
reached adulthood they would grow pink. And
the male dolphins tended to be pinker than the
females.

'Told you we'd see some!' said Barbara.

'This is incredible!' Evie's dad shouted, as all
six jumped out of the water together.

'It is very rare to see so many all at once,' said Ernesto. 'One or two, maybe, but six! It hardly ever happens! This is lucky! A lucky sign!'

Evie concentrated hard to pick up on what the dolphins were thinking and saying to each other.

'This is fun!' one said.

'Let's race the boat!' said another.

'I just ate a turtle,' said a third.

'I hate turtles! They get stuck in my teeth. Even worse than crabs.'

'No. Turtles are yum. Crunchy yumminess. And good for your teeth.'

'WHOOSH!' said another one, jumping through the air.

Evie tried to send a thought to them.

The thought wasn't a particularly deep or clever thought. It was:

'Hello! I am the human girl on the boat. Can you see me?'

The dolphins seemed confused by this.

'Did you hear something?' one asked.

'Um, I think I might have . . .'

And then the dolphins went quiet and disappeared out of sight, only to reappear moments later as they popped up beside the boat.

'Hello, human girl!'

'Yes, hello, human girl! What is that you are eating?'

'It's, um, a tacu tacu. It's human food. I don't think dolphins would like it.'

'Try us,' whistled one of the dolphins. The pinkest and largest with a few scratches on his face. They were quite a fighty species, Evie remembered reading.

So Evie shared out the delicious fried rice and bean dumpling with all six of the dolphins before her dad saw what she was doing.

'Evie! You can't do that!'

'Oops, better go!' said the large dolphin.

The dolphins disappeared. And Evie watched their pink bodies fade away into the river.

An hour later, they saw more jungle being destroyed.

They sailed past smoke and fire, and Evie heard the howling thoughts of howler monkeys as they scrambled across the canopies.

But then she heard a closer thought. Coming from the water's edge.

A slow, heavy thought.

'Help . . .

me . . .'

Evie saw a creature hanging from the low branch of a tree that was dangling over the water's edge. A strangely-shaped furry creature with a small head and long floppy limbs.

The Incredibly Daring Rescue

'Over there!' Evie pointed and shouted so Ernesto could hear. 'Over there! Look! A sloth. It needs our help.'

'She's right,' said Gerry, staring through his binoculars.

'There is no way we can reach it,' Ernesto said. 'Look! The fire is getting closer to the edge. And all the smoke. It is far too dangerous.'

Evie didn't like this. 'But we have to! It's in danger.'

'Yes,' said her dad, scratching his beard with his usual worried expression, 'and so would we be if we went over there. We have to keep moving down the river. The smoke is spreading. Evie, please.'

'Sloths can swim,' said Ernesto. 'They are actually great swimmers. It will be fine.'

But Evie could hear the thoughts of this particular sloth and realised it was too paralysed by shock to do anything.

'I . . .
what . . .
I . . .
don't . . .
I . . .' the sloth was thinking, with slow worry,
as it clung onto the branch of the tree.

Evie felt sad, and angry, and fear clasped her
brain like the sloth to the branch. And this fear
was the sloth's fear, which she felt almost as her
own.

And then a thought arrived in her head. It wasn't
her thought. It wasn't even the sloth's thought. It
was a thought from below. From the river.

'What's the matter?' the thought asked.

Evie peered over the side of the boat and saw
a flash of pink below the water's murky green
surface.

The river dolphin rose up and peered out into
the air. It was the large one she'd seen earlier.

'Listen, remember all that yummy food I gave
you?'

'Of course,' said the dolphin.

'Well, I need a favour . . . Look, see that animal
on the bank?'

'That freaky-looking thing?'

'Um, yes,' said Evie. 'That freaky-looking thing.

I'd like you to go and rescue her. I'll tell her to get on your back and then you bring her to the boat. Can you do that?'

The dolphin bobbed its head underwater, then came back above the surface. 'Do you have more food? I'll do it for more food.'

Evie turned and saw that Ernesto had an uneaten fried dumpling in his cabin. 'We do. And it's yours if you go over and save that sloth's life. She is really scared, and I don't think she will be able to swim. But you've got to be quick. The fire is spreading!'

The dolphin disappeared without another thought. Evie was worried. She had no idea if it was going to help or not, but as the seconds became minutes she thought all hope was lost.

But then she saw a bulbous pink dolphin head burst out of the water near the sloth.

'Get on his back, sloth!' Evie fired the thought like an arrow through the smoke-filled air. 'It's okay. It's okay. You're going to drop off the branch because that tree is going to burn soon. We are going to save your life!'

And the thought must have reached it because the sloth *very slowly* crawled further along the branch.

'Oh . . .

I . . .

must . . .

It's . . .

Oh . . .

high . . .

Here . . .

goes . . .'

And then —

Splash.

It dropped and flopped and splashed into the water.

'Oh no!' said Evie. 'She fell in!'

'Oh . . .

no . . .

I . . .

missed . . .'

'What's going on?' Ernesto asked.

'Evie is trying to save that sloth's life,' her dad explained. 'My daughter communicates with animals.'

Ernesto's eyes widened. He suddenly looked very excited. 'I knew it! I read about her. The story was in all the newspapers. Even in Peru, she is famous! I knew it! Ever since I saw her nodding at that giant otter we saw.'

Evie was hardly listening.

She was waiting to see the dolphin come out of the water again with the sloth on its back.

'I have never seen anything like this,' said Ernesto.

'Yes!' Evie shouted out loud.

As the dolphin and its load made its way towards the boat, Evie went into the ship's cabin.

'What are you doing?' Ernesto asked, confused.

'I am stealing your tacu tacu. You see, I bribed the dolphin.'

'Evie,' said her dad, 'you're not meant to steal things.'

But Ernesto laughed. 'It seems like a better cause than my big belly.'

And then the dolphin was there with the worried wet sloth still on its back.

'Be careful of her fingernails,' the dolphin warned. 'They're scratchy.'

Ernesto leaned over the boat and helped the sloth off the dolphin's back and onto the deck. The sloth looked up at Evie with sleepy eyes.

'Thank . . .

you . . .'

Evie smiled. 'Hey, it's okay. Let's get you dry. Come into the sun.'

A Sloth
Called Ah

The sloth was drying out in the sun as it clung on to Evie's back.

'Where . . .

has . . .

my . . .

home . . .

gone?' the sloth asked, in a thought of sleepy sadness.

'I am ashamed to say that my species, the humans, have destroyed it.'

'Why?'

'For money, mainly. And because some humans don't understand the importance of nature. Some of us seem to have forgotten that we are animals too. We need nature as much as you do.'

'What . . .

is . . .

money?'

'You're better off not knowing, to be honest.

By the way, I'm Evie,' said Evie. 'Do you have a name?'

'Yes . . .

my . . .

name . . .

is . . .

Ah.'

'Ah?' asked Evie.

'Yes.'

'Oh. Okay. Ah. I suppose a short name makes sense. What with you being a sloth. I mean, short names are quicker to say. And think.'

'What . . .

are . . .

you . . .

trying . . .

to . . .

say?'

'Nothing. Nothing. Never mind.'

'I . . .

am . . .

tired . . .'

'Ah,' said Evie.

'Yes?' said the sloth.

'No. I was just saying "ah" not "Ah". I say ah sometimes. I didn't mean Ah as in your name.'

'Ah,' said Ah.

And the sloth smiled with her eyes and Evie laughed.

A sloth joke.

Ah closed her eyes and fell asleep, and Evie and her dad carefully laid her down on a blanket.

'Just think, Dad, if we had gone to Mallorca we wouldn't have saved this sloth's life,' she told her dad.

'And we would have been entirely safe. Eating entirely safe churros on entirely safe beaches.'

'Safe is boring, Dad.'

'I like safe.'

The boat was now a good distance away from the fire and smoke.

'Is there anything we can do to stop this happening? All this destruction?' Evie asked Ernesto.

'It is very difficult. They keep clearing the land to make roads and farms. To plant soy or graze cattle. Cows! In the jungle! I like cows but the Amazon wasn't made for cows and greedy farmers. There are some laws that should protect the land, but they are broken all the time. The government doesn't care. They just care about money. It is a crime. They don't care about the tribes who live here. They don't care about the rainforest animals. They don't care about nature. And they don't care about the planet or the air we need to breathe. It is so sad.'

He looked close to tears.

'So, so sad,' said Barbara.

Evie's dad tried to comfort Ernesto.

'But there are people trying to stop this. Around the world. And especially here in South America. Isn't that true?'

Ernesto sighed. 'Yes, it is true. But it is a hard fight.'

Evie heard her dad tell Ernesto about her mum and she felt pride fill her body.

'Evie's mother and I used to live in another part of the rainforest. In Brazil. My wife was an incredibly brave woman. Her name was Anna Navarro. She dedicated her life to trying to look after animals and stop nature being destroyed.'

'She sounds like an amazing woman,' sighed Ernesto. 'And yes, there are people like her in Peru. Like Professor Abigail García.'

Evie raised both eyebrows. She knew that name.

'Professor Abigail García! Oh wow! Wow, wow. She is my hero. She is the author of *Animals of the Amazon*! It's my favourite book in the world.

I learned so many animal facts from it. And she has helped discover new species. Like the García monkey! She discovered that in 2011! They named a whole species after her.'

'Yes! That is her!' said Ernesto. 'She has a charity. It has a boring name – the International Centre for Rainforest Protection or something. But it does magical things. It is based in Iquitos City. They get money from the public and then buy parts of the rainforest.'

'What happens to the land after they've bought it?' asked Evie's dad.

Ernesto smiled. 'Nothing. Nothing at all. Which is the whole point. They let the jungle live. They stop it being burnt or logged or destroyed. They keep the animals safe.'

'That . . .

sounds . . .

wonderful,' said the sloth, waking up briefly, before yawning herself back to sleep on Evie's back.

Ah's tiredness was catching, and soon the passengers were all asleep along with the sloth while Ernesto yawned in the cabin. He managed to stay awake until morning, when they reached Iquitos City.

A Very
Grumpy Parrot

quitos City was a fantastic place. Maybe the most fantastic place Evie had ever been to in her entire life.

A whole city right in the midst of the rainforest, nestled beside the vast curving wonder of the Amazon River. And probably the only place in the world you could walk around with a sloth on your back and no one looked at you funny. They travelled in a three-wheeled tuk-tuk through the streets (a tuk-tuk is like a kind of multi-coloured scooter crossed with a car).

Motorbikes and rickshaws and pedestrians were everywhere. The buildings of the city were a variety of yellows and oranges and reds. They saw houses on stilts and kids in bare feet flying kites.

There was also a surprising number of street cats everywhere, staring as the traffic sped by.

There was no time for sight-seeing or cat-chatting, though.

Evie and her dad had decided to take Ah the sloth to Professor Abigail García at the International Centre for Rainforest Protection.

This had been Evie's idea. Because Evie really wanted to meet the author of her favourite book. But her dad had also agreed that the International Centre for Rainforest Protection would probably be the best place to take Ah as they would know the safest part of the jungle for the sloth to return to.

'They'll know what to do with her. And it's not like we can take her to England.'

'What . . .

is . . .

England?' asked Ah.

'It's a place without any jungles. Or wild sloths,' said Evie.

'It . . .

sounds . . .

terrible,' said the sloth.

'Well, that's a matter of opinion.'

Evie had imagined the International Centre for Rainforest Protection would be situated in a gleaming skyscraper, but it was very different.

It was a tiny wooden hut on stilts on the river. To reach it, you had to walk over planks of wood that formed a wooden walkway from the riverbank directly over the Amazon River itself. A rickety wooden street in the air.

Then there was an even thinner wonkier piece of wood that they had to walk on once they reached the little hut with the sign outside that said 'International Centre for Rainforest Protection' in three languages – Spanish, English and Quechua, which (according to Evie's dad) was a language spoken by the original people of Peru.

Ah was very still as Evie crossed the planks. And she was very careful not to scratch Evie with her claws. Evie balanced as they followed her dad over the thinner plank of wood to reach the International Centre for Rainforest Protection.

It was a small, humid wooden room. There was a ceiling fan but it didn't seem to be working. In the middle of the room was a large desk filled with an old computer and messy paperwork. Beside the desk was a bright red parrot with blue, green and yellow wings, sitting on a swing.

'A scarlet macaw!' Evie said excitedly. She tried to enter the macaw's head, but it turned out that parrots' heads (or this parrot at least) were filled with rude and angry thoughts that were hard to follow.

'Ssssh!' said her dad, pointing to a woman.

Professor Abigail García was on the telephone. She was shouting in Spanish.

Evie understood some of what she was saying.

'No, they can't do it! We must keep going! . . . We'll find the money! I don't know how, but we will . . . I don't know . . . I don't know . . . But we can't let the loggers take that land. We can't let them chop down a single rubber tree on that land. We just can't!'

Professor García put the phone down and slumped forward, exhausted, placing her face on the desk and swearing several times in Spanish. Ten swear words in total. Two of them so rude Evie had never actually heard them

before and Evie's dad quickly put his hands over her ears. Then she said another swear word that even Evie's *dad* hadn't heard before, and he seriously thought about covering his own ears.

'Wow,' he whispered, a little scared.

Evie noticed a large framed photograph of a jaguar on the wall.

Its spotted fur and ferocious jaws looked magnificent. She remembered that in *Animals of the Amazon* the first chapter had been about the jaguar. One of the deadliest predators in the jungle.

Professor García clearly hadn't seen the two humans and one sloth enter the small humid wooden office. But the scarlet macaw parrot perched on a swing near the roof was trying to tell her.

'Visitors!' she squawked. 'Visitors!'

At first Evie thought the noise was just the scarlet macaw's thoughts entering Evie's head, but then it became clear that the scarlet macaw was actually chirping it out loud.

'Neruda! *Silencio!*' said the professor, but the parrot – Neruda – kept squawking.

And then Professor García turned to the visitors and smiled wearily.

'*Hola*, hello . . . *buenos días*,' said Professor García, now in a quiet and tired voice.

'*Hola*. Hello. I am Santiago. And this is my daughter, Evie. And this is a sloth we rescued from the jungle.'

'That is interesting,' said Professor García, sounding like it was the least interesting thing she had ever heard. Evie couldn't help feeling she looked a lot older and tireder and sadder than the photo on the book cover.

'It's an honour to meet you,' said Evie, smiling.

'Ugh!' said Professor García, as if the words gave her a headache.

'She hates you,' thought Neruda.

'I read your book,' Evie went on. 'I learned so much. I learned that thirty-five species in the Amazon rainforest become extinct every day, and that rainfall has declined by 69 per cent since the year 2000, and that it contains one in ten species known on Earth and 40,000 species of plants. I learned that although many parts of the rainforest are jungle, not all are because the word "jungle" refers to the dense and tangled bits you can't walk around very easily. And I learned that Amazon wildlife is in great danger not just because—'

Professor García could take no more. 'Please. Stop.'

'I want to be like you.'

'Ugh. I don't even want to be like me.'

'But you're my hero. You found a new species of monkey!'

'Never meet your heroes,' said the professor, taking a swig from a hipflask.

'She doesn't like you,' thought Neruda. 'She really, really, really, really, really doesn't like you. She wants you to leave.'

'Well, that's rude!' Evie thought back.

The parrot jolted upright when she realised Evie could telepathically communicate with her and then she fell off her perch. Everyone looked at the parrot on the dusty floor. The bird quickly shook her feathers and flew back to her perch, looking intently at Evie. 'I'm okay, I'm okay,' she squawked, in parrot. 'I meant to do that.'

'We just wondered if you could help us,' Evie's dad said, turning his attention back to Professor García. 'You see, we wondered if your charity could find a new home for the sloth. A safe part of the jungle.'

'She's called Ah,' said Evie, as the sloth dribbled in her sleep.

Professor García looked like she could cry. 'I can, of course, take the sloth. I can place it in the jungle. But it won't be a safe part.'

'Why not?' Evie's dad asked. 'I thought that's what you did. You buy up land and you keep it safe.'

The professor sighed. 'Not any more. Nowhere is safe.'

'What happened?' asked Evie.

'We ran out of money. The land prices are rising and people have stopped giving us money. No one visits our website any more.'

Evie was confused. 'Why is the website so important?'

'The website is the easiest way for people to donate money! But it is a terrible website. It is the worst website in the whole history of websites. There is nothing on there that you couldn't find anywhere else. It's a really bad—'

The professor's eyes widened as she stared at Evie.

'*Espera!* Wait a minute! You! It's you! I know you. I have seen you . . .' She opened a drawer in her desk and rummaged around. Then she pulled out a copy of *Nature* magazine with Evie's face on it. 'Here! You are Evie Navarro. The animal talker!'

The Tingle in Evie's Head That Was the Start of a Brilliant Idea

'You are everywhere,' the professor said, her breath smelling stale. 'I saw a video on YouTube where you told a bearded dragon to change a TV channel, and one where you interviewed a seagull.'

'That was my idea,' Evie's dad said. 'The seagull. She wanted to interview a rattlesnake or a tarantula and I said, "Hey, maybe start with a seagull?"'

Professor García smiled. 'You are famous, Evie!'

'Also *annoying*,' thought Neruda.

'That's why we came here,' Evie told the professor, frowning at Neruda.

'Because you're annoying?' wondered Neruda. But Evie ignored her.

'It was getting a bit much at home so we came . . . here,' she said. 'I want to feel hopeful again.'

Professor García sighed, as if she was imitating the sloth. 'Well, I wish I could have given you that. Hope, I mean. But as of today, I have no hope. Tonight I'll shut down the website. And tomorrow I'll head back to the University of Lima and teach.'

She tore off a leaf from the plant on her desk and went over to give it to the sloth, who was waking up.

'Oh . . .

a . . .

leaf . . .

lovely . . .

yum,' said Ah.

'Look closely,' the professor said. 'Can you see that slight green tinge in her fur?'

Evie and her dad nodded.

'Is that bad?' asked Evie, worried.

'It's algae,' the professor explained, shaking her head. 'Algae grows on a sloth's fur. It evolved as a kind of camouflage. The sad thing is, no amount of camouflage can help a sloth nowadays. And sloths are homebodies. They like staying around the same trees. Peeing and pooping in the same place. They're not good at moving house. Or even moving toilet.' Professor García stroked the animal, and gently pulled it away from Evie.

'Oh . . .

this . . .

is . . .

new . . .

What . . .

is . . .

happening . . . ?'

'It's okay, Ah. The professor can help you.'

'I will take her back into the jungle. I will try to find the right home for her. But I can't promise she will be safe. I can't promise any animal will be safe from now on . . . You see, we have been trying to buy a piece of Amazon land near here. It is known as "the Monkey Lands" because of all the monkeys there. But there are sloths too. And jaguars.'

'Jaguars!' said Evie, excited.

'But the loggers have raised the price and we just can't afford it. We have no money.'

Evie nodded.

She wished she could do something to help the professor and the International Centre for Rainforest Protection.

But then she felt a small tingle of an idea.

She didn't know what the idea was yet, but the tingle was growing.

She looked down at her own face on the magazine.

She saw the headline.

'EVIE AND THE ANIMALS: HOW ONE BRITISH GIRL OFFERS THE KEY TO UNDERSTANDING THE NATURAL WORLD.'

She remembered what Professor García had said only a few moments before. About the website not being interesting enough.

'Right,' her dad was saying. 'We'll be on our way then. Back to England. I'm sorry there's nothing we can do to help.'

Evie was thinking really, really hard to work out what the tingle meant and then she had it. Just as they were walking out.

'Wait!' said Evie. 'There is! I mean, there might be. I've got an idea. And it just might work!'

The idea was simple. But also, genius.

That's what Professor García said.

'Genius.'

She actually used that word. Which made Evie blush.

'So, you are saying you would go into the jungle to do this?' she said.

'Yes. I would need you – or someone – to

take me into the rainforest and then I would interview different animals. About what it feels like to be them. And we could hear about rainforest destruction from their perspectives. They could tell me what they think about humans. And then we could write up the interviews and put them on your website and people would have to donate some money to read them.'

Professor García nodded, thinking. 'Yes. Just a donation. As large or small as they want. And I think it would be best if it was one animal at a time. But—'

'But what?' Evie wondered.

'But we would need to start with something good. Something exciting . . .' Professor García was pacing the room. She reached for her hipflask and raised it to her lips. She shook her head and threw it across the room, straight into the bin.

'Something safe,' Evie's dad volunteered. 'Like an otter?'

But then Evie gazed at the picture of the jaguar again. 'Him! I want to interview him!'

And Professor García smiled. 'I've always wanted to know what he's thinking.'

Four Mosquitoes and a Poison Dart Frog

E vie was hot. And sweaty. And had been bitten by a hundred mosquitoes.

The mosquitoes were still around her. 'Blood,' said one. 'Give me blood.'

'Over here,' said another. 'This girl here. The best blood around.'

'Oh yes, this is exquisite blood,' said a third, biting into Evie's arm. 'So many flavours. I'm getting hints of blackberry and juniper.'

'Give me some of that,' said yet another, as Evie tried to swat it away. 'Oh no! Quick! She is fast with her hands. Mayday, mayday! Abort mission! Repeat – ABORT MISSION! Get out of here, guys . . .'

The humans had walked for miles. Deep into what was now most definitely jungle. The Monkey Lands. Evie, her dad, Professor García and two local trackers, who led the way armed with infinite knowledge and machetes they used to cut through the undergrowth.

Evie gazed up at the sky but could hardly see it, as it was lost beneath a thick canopy of trees. She looked at the ground and saw beautiful star-shaped white Amazon lilies.

'This is one of the very deadliest parts of the jungle,' said Pihlo, the tracker in front, smiling as if the deadliest part of the jungle was kind of fun. 'Look! Right there!'

He pointed at a bright yellow frog sitting quietly on a leaf.

Evie knew exactly what type of frog this was. She'd had a memory dream about a similar frog many times. When she had been a little child with her parents living in the Amazon, she had apparently seen many of them.

It was a poison dart frog. It had enough poison on its skin to kill twenty men. But Evie also knew that it wasn't *venomous*. Meaning it didn't go out of its way to bite you and transmit poison

that way, like a snake. It just killed you if you licked it or touched it or tried to eat it.

'Stay away,' the creature – a female – thought.

'Don't worry. We're not going to hurt you.'

'Oh, that's good. For you, I mean.'

'I know. You're poisonous.'

'Yep,' said the frog, laughing. 'I am the deadliest. I am a mean green killing machine.'

'You're not green,' said Evie, with her mind.

'I know. But it rhymes. I mean, what rhymes with yellow? Mellow? Come on!'

'I understand,' said Evie.

Evie asked everyone to stop so she could do a little interview, for later use. Professor García agreed, although Evie's dad thought it a bad idea. 'Evie, that frog is *literally* the most poisonous animal in the world.'

'Can it be a *quick* interview?'

And it was.

Evie discovered that the poison dart frog was actually quite a sad creature who felt bad most of the time for killing anything that it touched.

'It's a lot of guilt. It's terrible. It haunts my dreams. All the bodies.'

Evie learned that the frog sang sad songs to itself all day long. One of the songs was called

'Beautiful Poison'. ('It's a masterpiece. If I do say so myself.')

Shortly after the encounter with a frog, they saw a tree snake. The snake definitely wasn't in the mood for an interview – 'Not today, sssssssssstay away' – so they carried on, continually checking the ground for any potentially deadly spiders. They saw lots of monkeys (these were the Monkey Lands, after all). And the monkeys told the rudest jokes Evie had ever heard. Far too rude to repeat on Professor García's website.

And then, suddenly, they saw it.

Lurking near a small clearing between the trees.

A jaguar.

Maybe the exact same jaguar from the photo hanging in Professor García's office.

Large and sleek.

Golden coat with black spots.

(The spots weren't really spots. More like little roses. In fact, as Evie knew, they were actually called 'rosettes', these markings. And they helped make the jaguar one of the most formidable-looking creatures on the planet.)

'Okay,' Evie said to the others. 'You all stay back. I will go and talk to it.'

'I think this is a bad idea,' said Evie's dad, shaking his head.

'It will be fine. Honestly, Dad, it will be fine.' She hugged him.

Her dad shrugged in defeat. 'Why didn't we just go to Cornwall?' he wondered. 'It's nice in Cornwall. We could be having an ice cream on the beach . . .'

'Dad, trust me. I've got this.'

An Interview
with a Jaguar

Evie stepped forward, past the professor and the guides, towards the jaguar.

'Don't come any closer,' the jaguar said. 'Or I'll kill you.'

Evie didn't take long to think about this. 'Okay. I'll stay right here. Look, I'm not moving any further.'

The jaguar tilted his head to one side, like a curious kitten. 'How are you doing that? None of the others can do that.'

'Doing what?'

'Getting inside my head. It's strange. Kind of tickles.'

'It's just a skill I have.'

'Ah, skills. *Skills.* I also have skills,' said the jaguar. 'Like I could jump from here and land on you with my jaws wide open and kill you, just like that. I wouldn't even break into a sweat. And it would be beautiful.'

Evie's mouth felt suddenly dry. She turned

back and saw her dad's worried face shadowed by trees. 'That's, um, really good to know.'

The jaguar licked his paw.

'I don't like your kind,' said the jaguar. 'I have seen what you are doing to this place. Destroying it. I have seen the fires. I have seen the machines. I have seen my home disappear. Your kind destroys. That's what you do.'

Evie nodded. She doubted jaguars understood nodding but she nodded anyway. 'Yes. I know. Humans are destroying this place. This is why I am here. This is why I want to talk to you. You see, there are humans who don't care about the rainforest but there are also a lot of humans who do. And that number is growing. All the time.'

'That is a very interesting story,' said the jaguar sarcastically, with a yawn that revealed his long teeth.

Evie scratched a mosquito bite on her arm. 'No, it really is. You see, some humans now understand that saving the jungle and all the creatures who live here is good for everybody in the world. This rainforest not only helps make rain, which is good for everything, but it captures a lot of carbon dioxide. And it produces oxygen.

Which helps everyone and everything alive on this planet.'

The jaguar scratched his ear with a rear paw. 'That's a lot of very long words. Could you explain it more simply? I've had a long day. I have done a LOT of prowling. It takes it out of you.'

'Um, well – we want you to be able to have a home. And more people will want to protect your home if we know more about you. And as I have the ability to "talk" with you, it seemed like a good idea that I do that, and tell people about the world from a jaguar's perspective. So then they would understand you, and like you, and be more likely to protect your home. Do you see?'

The jaguar stopped scratching his ear. Placed his paw on the ground. 'Hmmm. Interesting. Will you be talking to any other animals too?'

'Yes.'

The jaguar looked a little upset by this, and turned to walk away through the dense undergrowth.

'But you're the main one. The first interview. The most important.'

The jaguar stopped. 'Most important, you say?'

'Absolutely. The first. For the website . . .' She was going to explain what a website was but realised it was impossible. 'It's quite a big deal. And humans will get to understand you more. And give money – a very important human thing.'

'That's good. Because I *am* a big deal.'

'Exactly.'

The jaguar turned and started walking back. Towards Evie. Evie tried to stay calm and ignore the fact that he was licking his lips. She stayed totally still.

The spotted creature sat down right in front of her. 'All right then. Ask me a question.'

Evie was now talking out loud as well as thinking. Talking was a way for her to think clearly, when she was nervous. 'Right, right, okay . . .'

She pulled a notepad out of her bag.

'Is that a gun?' snarled the jaguar.

'No. It's paper. You scratch things on it with this thing, called a pen. The things are called words. They mean things to humans. I am going to write down what you are thinking.'

'Hmmm. Okay. So, ask me something.'

'Do you have a name?'

'No. Our kind doesn't have names. We are part

of the world around us. We are not separate. There is no divide between things. Names are foolish. You are foolish. Next question.'

'Um, okay. Well, what is it like to be you? What does it feel like?'

The jaguar considered. 'Great. Yeah. Great. It feels great.'

'Why?'

'Because I am in charge. Look at me, I'm the biggest animal in the world.'

Evie grimaced. She looked at the power of his jaw. His taut muscles and the energy in his body. She really didn't want to disagree with him. But, well, facts were facts. 'Actually, that's the blue whale.'

'The blue what?'

'It's a sea creature. Far away from here. Under the water, mostly. That is the biggest animal in the world.'

The jaguar huffed. And then growled. 'How *DARE* you?'

'I mean you are exactly as big as you need to be. And blue whales are totally overrated.'

'You don't believe that,' said the jaguar.

Evie nodded. She knew she couldn't hide her thoughts. 'You are totally right. Blue whales are

EPIC. Did you know that they are related to hippos and evolved from land animals? Isn't that great! And their tongue alone can weigh as much as an elephant! And yes, I know you don't know what an elephant or a hippo is and you probably don't have a clue what "evolved" means but, trust me, these are *AMAZING FACTS*. And a blue whale's mouth can fit a hundred humans inside. A hundred.'

'I could do that,' said the jaguar. 'Not all at once. But over time. It would be a fun challenge.' He thought of something. 'All right, then I am not the size of a blue whale but at least I am the biggest *cat* in the world.'

Evie shook her head. 'Actually, that would be the tiger. The Siberian tiger to be specific.'

'The *what*?'

'I'll show you.'

And Evie closed her eyes and thought really hard and pictured a tiger.

'Ah, I see it,' said the jaguar, admiring the clever telepathic mind trick. 'What an ugly beast. Whoever thought stripes would be a good look?'

'And then after the tigers it's the lion. That's number two.'

Evie imagined a male lion for him to see.

'That's funny. All that hair around its face.'

'It's a mane.'

'It's ridiculous. That's what it is. He looks like a furry sun.'

'Okay. Well, humans talk a lot about lions. But if you give me a great interview maybe they will talk more about jaguars.'

'Hmmm. Okay. What do you want me to tell you?'

Evie smiled. And the interview got underway.

There was noise everywhere. Buzzing insects. Chirping frogs. The deep distant roar of howler monkeys. But right there in the clearing her focus was on nothing but the jaguar's thoughts entering her head. And she began to communicate with the creature at a deep level.

The jaguar revealed its dreams. It revealed its nightmares too. Like the one in which he relived the day his sister was shot by a human.

He told Evie he liked swimming. And that it was only during swimming and hunting that he felt truly free, truly alive. His favourite food was armadillo. ('You should try it. Salty and delicious.') But he also liked the taste of anteaters. ('So good.') He had never attacked a human and sensed they wouldn't be tasty. He liked to sleep a lot during the day and to feel awake during the 'comfort of night'. And he loved to be alone.

His advice for humans was simple. Take from the world only what you need. Because only then can you be happy with what you have.

'Life becomes heavy, otherwise. Tread as lightly as air and stay in tune with nature, because that's the only song we really have.'

And she was writing it all down as fast as she could. And then Evie's dad said, nervously, from the trees, 'Evie, it's going to get dark soon. We had better get back.'

It was, Evie had to admit, a great interview.

'I agree,' thought the jaguar. 'And I don't even know what an interview is.'

The jaguar came close. Evie stroked his head. 'If you had one request for humans, what would it be?'

'You are destroying my home and you don't need to. Please stop.'

'Thank you,' she said.

'Will this stop humans trying to destroy our home?'

Evie smiled. 'Well, it will be a start.'

Evie Saves
the Jungle

The interview was put on the internet.

And the story was in newspapers around the world.

From the *Peru Tribune* to the *Lofting Evening Post*.

And so Evie was even more famous than ever.

'Wow! You're bigger than Ed Sheeran,' her friend Ramesh texted. 'You should make a song! I could play guitar. You could be a star. You could *be* Ed Sheeran.'

'Ramesh!' she texted back from her bed at Professor García's house. 'You are forgetting one thing. I don't want to be Ed Sheeran.'

But the truth was, this time Evie didn't mind being famous.

If being a bit famous could help save the Amazon rainforest and Professor García's charity it was worth it.

And within a week they had raised enough

money to stop the loggers buying the Monkey Lands. Which meant the jaguar was safe.

And within a month they had raised ten million sol. Sol was the type of money in Peru. And ten million was a lot of it.

Professor García made them tacu tacu every night.

'You know you came into my office and said I was your hero? Well, you are *my* hero. You are the greatest hero of all time. You have saved the charity. You have saved parts of the jungle. You are a jungle saviour!'

During that month Evie interviewed a lot of animals.

She interviewed the pink river dolphin who had saved Ah's life.

She interviewed Ah. It took a long time. Seventeen hours and fifty-seven minutes and forty-four seconds. But they got there in the end.

She interviewed Neruda the scarlet macaw. Well, she *tried* to interview Neruda but Neruda was so rude it was quite tricky. Every time Evie tried to ask Neruda something the thought came back: 'No comment. Except I hate you. I mean like *really.*' And then she did a poo on Evie's head.

Evie interviewed squirrel monkeys and howler monkeys and toucans and tarantulas and an anaconda and weird and wonderful Amazonian creatures like a capybara, the largest rodent in the world, which had reddish brown fur and – Evie thought – a somewhat weird barrel-shaped body and a strange short head. Though the cabypara didn't like these thoughts.

'My body is not weird and my head is not strange. How dare you!'

She even interviewed a mosquito. But only after she agreed to let the mosquito bite her five times. And the only thing the mosquito wanted to talk about was the taste of her blood.

One night they FaceTimed Granny Flora. As Evie's dad chatted to Granny Flora, Evie had a mind-chat with Scruff.

'I've had pizza every day for breakfast!'

'Pizza is not good for dogs, Scruff.'

'Well, the heart wants what it wants. And my heart wants pizza.' Scruff licked his paw, a little embarrassed. 'But it also wants you. I have missed you. The tummy rubs, mainly. And that weird smell you've got.'

'Hey! What weird smell?'

'Don't worry. No human would notice.'

After the chat was over, they went to sit outside. Evie told her dad she thought it was time to go home. 'School will be starting soon. And it would be nice to have a few full days with Scruff before going back.'

Her dad looked very relieved. 'Yes, good idea. Very good idea. Let's go home. You have helped the charity and they will raise more and more money now. It is time to go back.'

Evie smiled as her dad hugged her.

'Mum would have been so proud,' he said.

Evie felt a tear form in her eye. A tear of sadness and happiness. She stared at the sloth in the hammock, sleeping under a clear night sky of a million stars.

'You were right,' her dad said. 'This was the place to come. We can do Mallorca or Cornwall another year.'

Evie smiled. 'Thank you, Dad. Thanks for letting me look after animals.'

'I only worry.'

She stared at her dad's face and wished there was a way for him to worry less about things. 'There was something the jaguar told me,' she said. 'Everything is connected. There is no divide between him and the rest of nature. I mean, looking after animals, looking after nature, that *is* looking after yourself. Because we *are* nature. We *are* animals. And this world is the only home we've got.'

They sat there a while. Listening to the chirping of crickets. Evie's dad was going to say something else. Another worry. But he saw the smile on his daughter's face and decided he wanted it to stay there. The smile.

'I want to interview other animals,' Evie said. 'Not just jungle ones.'

'Phew,' her dad said. 'Jungle ones are dangerous.

So what animal do you want to interview next?'

Evie took a moment to think. 'Hmmm. I was thinking . . . a *shark*.'

Her dad went pale. And Evie started to laugh, and then her dad laughed, and they both kept laughing until they realised it was probably time for bed.

THE END

Character fact files

Evie Santiago

Evie is kind and brave and cares about creatures and the environment. She is also unlike other children – she can speak to animals and understand what they are saying. You can read more about her adventures in *Evie and the Animals*.

Pink River Dolphin

The pink river dolphins in this book love jumping next to Evie's boat and whooshing about making massive splashes. Pink river dolphins are really special – they make their home in rivers, can only be found in South America and get their name because they are a lovely pink colour!

Neruda the Scarlet Macaw

Neruda is so rude that when Evie tries to interview her, she poos on Evie's head! Scarlet macaws are the biggest species of parrot in the world and their beak is super-strong so that they can crack open the nuts they eat.

Scruff

Scruff became friends with Evie when she fixed his sore paw in *Evie and the Animals*. He loves Evie, tummy rubs and pizza. He also really likes Evie's Granny Flora as she can speak to animals too AND lets Scruff sleep in her bed.

....

Jaguar

The Jaguar in this book is a truly magnificent creature, and he knows it! He is proud and thinks he is better than everyone else. He also loves swimming, comes out mostly at night and eats things like armadillos and fish.

....

Ah
the Three-toed Sloth

Evie rescues Ah from a rainforest fire and they become friends. Ah the sloth is clever and funny, even though she is only able to move and speak very slowly. Three-toed sloths are the slowest mammals on the planet and their 'toes' are actually really strong claws.

Find out how Evie's

ADVENTURES

began . . .

FROM BESTSELLING AUTHOR

Matt Haig

A Wild Adventure

Evie and the ANIMALS

Illustrated by Emily Gravett

Read on for an extract from
EVIE AND THE ANIMALS

The Snake
and the Frog

T hat night Evie had a dream.

The dream wasn't about a rabbit. It wasn't even about Granny Flora or a circus or a prison. It was about a snake.

A tree snake.

A tree snake on one of those low, twisty trees that you find deep in the jungle.

It wasn't an anaconda, because it wasn't in or around a river. But it was green. Bright green. It was a bright green emerald tree boa. Evie knew that. She knew that it could kill, not with venom but by crushing or, if its prey was small enough, biting.

And it had spotted something on the ground.

A frog. This frog was also brightly coloured. It was bright blue and black. It was the prettiest frog ever. It was a poison dart frog. Evie had read that they contained more poison than the Brazilian wandering spider, so were arguably the deadliest creature in the whole Amazon. She knew that they wouldn't hurt you if you left them alone, but that their skin was coated in enough poison to kill ten grown men.

She felt scared about the snake. Not scared *of* it, but *for* it. If it touched the frog it would die. And the frog might die too.

Without thinking, she urged the snake not to touch it.

'*It will kill you.*'

And just then the snake stopped looking at the frog and looked at little Evie instead. But in this dream Evie wasn't at all scared.

'If you even touch that frog, you will be dead,' Evie said, with her mind.

She felt the snake inside her head. She could hear the snake's thoughts. 'It looks plump. It looks tasty.'

'No,' Evie told the snake. 'It is deadly. It is a poison dart frog. You are still a very young snake. You don't understand these things.'

The snake was confused. 'Why do you want to save me?'

Even in a dream Evie found this an easy question to answer. 'Because I can.'

She knew that both the snake and the frog could kill her, but that didn't mean she wanted them dead.

'Thank you,' thought the snake. 'You are a good human. Not like Mortimer.'

'Mortimer?'

'He is after me. He is trying to control me. He is not like you. Or your parents.'

Evie watched the poison dart frog hop away underneath a log. Then she turned her attention back to the snake. 'You know my parents?'

'Yes, they are right there.'

And the tree snake slid back up the tree and out of her thoughts and, in the dream, Evie turned around and saw her parents. She was the height of a toddler in this dream, so they towered above her. Her dad looked younger and happier and he had no beard. And her mum looked as kind and warm as she did in the photo.

'Mum!' she said. And she tried to hug her. But that was where the dream ended.

When she woke up, she had a very weird feeling.

As though the dream hadn't really been a dream at all.

It had felt, in fact, like a memory.

You may not be able to talk to animals like Evie but there are other ways that YOU can help the planet and the creatures that live in it!

1 Turn the lights out. Whenever you leave a room, make sure that the lights are switched off. This includes turning off any machines like a television at the wall. If you can still see a tiny light after you have turned an electrical item off, it means the machine is on 'standby' and is still using electricity.

2 Recycle plastic, cardboard, paper, aluminium and glass where you can. If you're not sure if you can recycle it or not, look out for this little symbol that is on most recyclable products. ♻

3 Pass on your toys. Have you grown out of your toys? Perhaps you don't enjoy playing with them so much any more? Another child might love what you don't want so you could donate any unwanted toys to a charity shop or local family.

4 Try to walk to where you need to go rather than always getting in the car with your family. You will see so much more wildlife if you walk and it could be a nice way to spend time together outside in nature.

5 Take care with water. Although it's lovely to have a soak in a deep, warm bath, a quick shower uses much less water so try to mix it up. You could also turn the tap off when you are brushing your teeth.

MORE FROM

Matt Haig

WORLD
BOOK
DAY

SHARE
A STORY

Well **hello** there! We are

Overjoyed that you have **joined our celebration** of

Reading books and **sharing stories**, because we

Love bringing **books** to you.

Did you know, we are a **charity** dedicated to celebrating the

Brilliance of **reading for pleasure** for everyone, everywhere?

Our mission is to help you discover **brand new stories** and

Open your mind to exciting **new worlds** and **characters**, from

Kings and **queens** to **wizards** and **pirates** to **animals** and **adventurers** and so many more. We couldn't

Do it without all the amazing **authors** and **illustrators**, **booksellers** and **bookshops**, publishers, **schools** and **libraries** out there –

And most importantly, we couldn't do it all without . . .

YOU!

On your bookmarks, get set, READ!
Happy Reading. Happy World Book Day.

Rob Biddulph

SHARE A STORY

From breakfast to bedtime, there's always time to discover and share stories together. You can . . .

1 TAKE A TRIP to your LOCAL BOOKSHOP

Brimming with brilliant books and helpful booksellers to share awesome reading recommendations, you can also enjoy booky events with your favourite authors and illustrators.

 FIND YOUR LOCAL BOOKSHOP: booksellers.org.uk/ bookshopsearch

2 JOIN your LOCAL LIBRARY

That wonderful place where the hugest selection of books you could ever want to read awaits – and you can borrow them for FREE! Plus expert advice and fantastic free family reading events.

FIND YOUR LOCAL LIBRARY: gov.uk/local-library-services/

3 CHECK OUT the WORLD BOOK DAY WEBSITE

Looking for reading tips, advice and inspiration? There is so much for you to discover at **worldbookday.com**, packed with fun activities, games, downloads, podcasts, videos, competitions and all the latest new books galore.

SPONSORED BY

Rob Biddulph